# Journey To The Depth Of Soul

-DHRUV SHAH

# SPECTRUM OF THOUGHTS

AM/56, Basanti Colony, Rourkela 769012, Odisha

**A Unit of FANATIXX PUBLICATION.**

**Website:** www.fanatixx.in



**"Journey To The Depth Of Soul"** by: **DHRUV SHAH**

ISBN: **978-93-89557-46-6**

FICTION STORIES 1st Edition

Book Formatting: Mayuri Valanju

Cover Design: Sagar Samal

# Disclaimer

This is a work of fiction. The compiler has tried their best to edit and curate the content of the co-authors and has been made plagiarism free.

All the write-ups in this book are unique.

In case if any plagiarism is detected, neither the compiler nor the publishers are responsible. Co-authors will be responsible for the content they have submitted.

# Acknowledgement

The making of this anthology wouldn't have been possible without the co-authors. A sincere gratitude to all those who've given their sincere time and effort to make this book a real success.

I also want to convey my gratitude to Fanatixx Publications without whom this project would not have been possible.

Above all, I heartily thank our parents, family and friends for supporting us throughout this wonderful journey.

Lastly, we thank the almighty for giving us this opportunity and strength to completing this precious project.

# Contents


SPECTRUM OF THOUGHTS.............. 1

Disclaimer....................... 2

Acknowledgement.................. 3

Dhruv Shah....................... 7

Aayushi Turakhia................. 8

Sleepless Nights................. 9

Ocean of thoughts................ 10

Me & My Soul..................... 10

A NIGHT.......................... 11

A few dreams to live............. 12

You.............................. 12

Passion.......................... 13

Friendship....................... 14

Dark Sky Night................... 15

Away to nature................... 17

A Place.......................... 18

DEVIL............................ 20

Dhruvi........................... 21

Waves............................ 22

Drishti Sapru.................... 29

Solitude......................... 30

Ishani Bali...................... 59

Lisha Desale.................... 67

Fond Mothers, Dr. Strange and a
Loving Partner.................... 68

Anger and patience : She gave me
the best.................... 73

Roses.................... 80

Mritika Mazumder.................... 83

The sexiest thing about smoking. 84

Two shots of whiskey fall in love
with five shots of vodka........ 86

Gender discrimination........... 88

Fate of our love................ 89

Nishita M. Agath................ 91

Saramitra.................... 102

Escapade.................... 103

I Set You Free.................... 104

What Gives You The Right?...... 105

To Be You!.................... 106

My Master.................... 107

Breathe!.................... 109

PAIN.................... 111

A Bloody Roar.................... 112

True Friends.................... 113

Sunit Agarwal.................... 114

An open letter to my best friend.
.............................. 116

HUMANITY......................... 117

Karma!........................... 121

My 2am thoughts.................. 121

I'm a total mess up.............. 123

# Dhruv Shah

Instagram Id: thoughtfull_writes

Admin of ink_that_never_fades and quotestation. He is an ambivert who likes to travel a lot and to observe new things. He connects with people and strikes interesting

conversations with everyone. He can be quite influential and has lasting impression on people's opinions. He is studying for BCOM and plans to do MBA and has further business plans. He strongly believes that one never gets more than one's luck and efforts.

# Aayushi Turakhia

Instagram Id: aayu_turakhia

A girl from Mumbai, following her dreams... Fashion designer by profession and B.Com by graduation and Writer by passion...

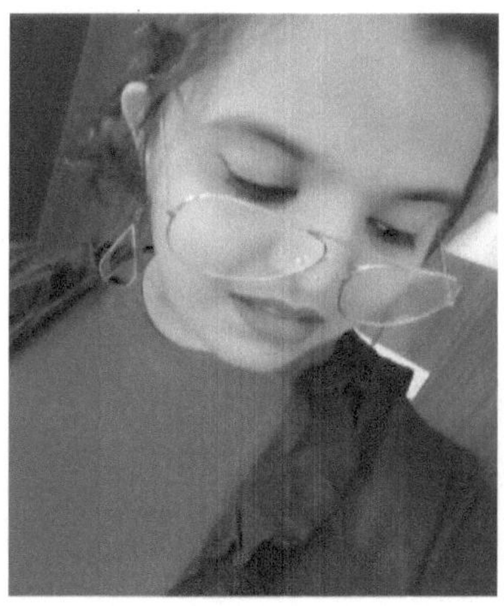

Here she is today, Aayushi Turakhia, by name... just a teenager living in for today...

# Sleepless Nights

Sleepless eyes at night,

A weird feeling in heart

and Mind traveling a few places...

Her to-do list became endless,

her mind ran to the far most
future,

her plans and her goals,

replaced her blood...

Here, at this very point of night
light,

she took her books in her own
hands...

She decided to create her own
story,

And write her own future...

To follow a role model is easy,

but to be one, is what the
challenge is...

And she prepared herself,

to accept that challenge...

Because that's what makes

her heart smile a bit brighter.

* * * *

## Ocean of thoughts

A ocean of thoughts have filled my
mind,
From which a river is flowing
through my veins...
Only a lake can be spoken out loud,
And a pond can be explained...
And I end up saying just a few
drops to you...

* * * *

## Me & My Soul

Sitting on the sea shore...

The movement of waves...

The blinking of stars...

The peace it leads me too...

These beating of my heart beats...

The perfect tune it makes...

Silencing all the moving traffic...

Its just me and my soul,

talking and thinking out loud...

This lighting of the street
lights...

Leading me to my thoughts...

Its just me and my soul,

Talking and thinking out loud.

★ ★ ★ ★

# A NIGHT

A night just like a regular one...
Under the moon and the stars,
With your fingers inter-twined with
mine...
With our backs on that trickling
sand or wet grasses,
With our heart beats being our
music...
With our silence being our harmony,
With our souls being one...
Would turn it into a very special
one for US to remember...

# A few dreams to live

A few dreams to live,
A bucket list to tick,
A bunch of friends to meet,
A lane of memories to visit,
A dark night to see,
A bright light to find,
A few dreams to live.

****

# You

Accusing, denying..
I can't imagine a world with you
gone...
The joy and the chaos, the demons
we're made of...
I'd be lost, if you left me
alone...
Hold on, I still want you...
Come back, I still need you...
Let me take your hand, I'll make it
right...
I swear to love you all my life...
Hold on, I still need you...

# Passion

In today's hectic life,

It's not so easy to follow our
passion...
Everyone is running a race,

while others are preparing
themselves to join the crowd...
We barely get time to even sleep,

how are we suppose to make time, to
follow our passion...?
We then steal seconds and minutes,

here and there,

and work towards our passion..
Away from all the crowd,

away from all the races,

away from reality...
We leave for a search,

of ourselves,

and work towards,

what inspires us, motivates us,

our passion...!

# Friendship

Friendship has its own unique
flavour,

Its own different hangover...

Where madness has its own twist...

Where craziness and mental illness
takes birth...

I bond where if one is happy,

we all go crazy...

But where one is sad...

All the rest of the gang gets
upset...

Friends together are that beautiful
dream, where nothing is yours and
nothing is mine...

Friendship has its own unique
flavour,

Its own different hangover...

# Dark Sky Night

In the dark sky night,

A lone dull road,

A few moments of tear,

A few butterflies of fear…

She walked alone

the path of death,

She screamed alone

the life of hell…

 From learning to fighting

The most we learned was as a kid...

Getting old

just got us stuck up

with the society and social mess...

Being a kid and learning new stuff

was all fun and laughter,

Learning stuff as adults

is all maturity and sacrifices...

Or the fight we lead as a disturbed
adult...

A fight with our wishes,

A fight with our hopes,

A fight with our dreams,

A fight with a society we live
in...

# Away to nature

When whole world around us was gossiping,

The colours of the sky,

The sound of waves hitting those stones,

Took her Away from the gossips,

Away from the reality,

To her wonder land,

Where the lights were the directions,

The road was her way,

Moon was the map,

Breeze was her AC,

And nature was her song…

# A Place

A place away from

all the hassles and races of the
city...

A place away from

all the worries and problems of the
city...

A place away from

all the haters and lovers...

A place away from

all the crimes and rules...

A place of peace...

A place of Haven...

A place of pleasure...

A place of life...

A place of warmth...

A place beneath the stars...

A place besides the Ocean...

A place where the Wind addresses...

A place even the Sun kisses...

A place to myself...

A place of mine...

A place I call Home...

★★★★

# DEVIL

Angel's Devil

Demon he was,

Pure soul she became...

No soul is pure,

But at least

better then the demon

she became...

Boiling blood within

was his habit,

And cooling down,

Was her passion...

Calming the demon within,

Was her aim...

But demon is demon,

Time is the wait...

The change took its time,

But the persistence shined,

Angel's devil was now his name...

# Dhruvi

21

Instagram Id: bleeding_poetry_

Hey my name is Dhruvi, I'm 18 and from Gujarat. I have a huge respect and love for poetries and for the poets round the globe.

# Waves

Crashing against rocks, splashing around my feet, cool than my pale skin and refreshing every cell as it runs around.
How ferocious they are while they arise, shaking the air above them, I wonder who would be creating this enormous energy, I bend down to see but end up with my own contorted reflection. My face reflection in water, distorted yet calm and something I looked at happily. The thoughts of someone creating the turbulent waves almost vanished as there was silence and stillness deep down at the ocean bed. Where all shall return there once to sleep, until our bones shatter and the ocean will bleed.

********

This pain I feel deep down in my chest, simply numbness flowing through the veins, taking everything with it and messing up before I could do anything about it. Somethings have hit me like a storm hitting an island on a warm good day, like suddenly there's everything fading to nothing. This simple endings to stories I wish I wanted to hear, endings of some relationships.When I wanted it to cherish for the rest, endings to some feelings good and bad, and most importantly an ending to the better self of my own. But this doesn't stop here, the world doesn't stop here, the people whom you love and the one who hardly cares about you, no it doesn't stop here. There's lot you'll face and you'll see. And then you may feel pain in a different way, like I do, its just the feeling of loneliness in your bones that makes you feel alive.

********

This thought in my mind unwraps today, like a newly fresh bud of rose spreading its colour into the black and white world, come on lets spend this one eternal life together! Let's turn on the radio and dance on our favourite songs like there's never a tomorrow, lets go on a road trip where the way takes us to a place where we can scream our love into those calm air. Come on lets walk together on a beach and make sand castles like a kid while clicking some beautiful memories and laughters in our eyes for the rest of our lives. Come on lets see those sunsets for a while, let me lean on your shoulders and let me see the beauty of hues of sky. Let me love you for a little while. While I smile at this thought right now, I hope you remember me wherever you are today.

**★★★★**

I still remember that night when you left me alone , in the dark , I was crying and hoping that you did stay just for one last time. Because there's so much you need to know about me and also how much I love and care for you. With all of your imperfections, and mine too, I still want us to be in the end. How easily I did think this and how easily you shattered all of my fantasies into just simple nothings. That night, I felt scary and that feeling of emptiness hit me hard that it shook my concept of love. At that moment I felt loving someone is just a fake thing and there is no such thing called love in this entire universe. How challenging it was for me to make my mind understand that you never needed me nor you will. And with all this pain you gave me, I still wish that may you never come across a scenario like mine where you have to just walk away from someone's life just because you truly love them.

********

A woman's body is where the life is nurtured, I place where strength runs in veins , grace in minds and care in their hearts ,
A place where woman feels loved , contented and sheltered
I body which tells stories about its survival, its pain , losses , struggles, and its existence.
Growing every second , facing nature, careless criticism , male chauvinism , patriarchy, body shaming and standing strong,
And still standing strong and robust, ready to face anything with audacity
This few inches of skin absorbs all

that universe offers and radiates
light which helps moon glow during
the darkest nights. It gives birth
to stars, moon and souls and fire,
water, air are its elements , those
progenitors of Earth is the one
which a woman's body is made of,
and here it is to create, maintain
and destroy whatever that's coming
in her way.

When we look back into the past ,
we come to know how deep and dark
it is and in all matters, and that
even our own mind fears to look
back at.

**★★★★**

Walking through the dark lane, my
eyes stuck on the most beautiful
creation of the nature, the moon.
It was beaming warm red, its warmth
I felt deep down in my chest.
Holding hands with the man of my
life and walking together through
that dark lane and singing our
favourite song all the while, I
can't tell how beautiful and caring
I felt that night. The crescent
moon, the crickets chirping, the
dark green bushes along the way,
the calm air, and the sweet smell

of the flowers nearby, all lifted
me up, gave some meaning and light
to my dark monotonous nights.

**★★★★**

Some wounds cut you deep and they
can't be filled with love or
stitched with care.

**★★★★**

We are all a tired soul behind a
beating heart and a bright smile.

**★★★★**

 3 a.m. seems so empty with so much
presence of yours.

It feels like I'm going on a path
where past is blurry and future is
ineffable.

**★★★★**

 See the power of your love, even
roses grow near your grave , and
see the power of my heart its still
holding up brave.

**★★★★**

 Your love symbolizes
rhododendrons, daisies and a

hundred leaved roses Pure, attached
and never ending.

★★★★

On this nascent evening while I sit
on the chair outside in my garden,
a dead pansy flower rolls into my
hand. I look at it and felt
romantic about the way it was lying
on my palm. The trust it had on me
that I would never crush it into
simple nothings, did left me
falling in love with a dead flower.
And this is how I loved death with
all of my heart.

★★★★

The way your hands fit in mine and
the way your lucid eyes stares me
every night, I fear the moon will
never set and will revere us
forever.

★★★★

Come here for a while and let me
love you again, and this time
surely forever.

★★★★

# Drishti Sapru

Instagram Id: mend._

Drishti Sapru is 22 years old. She loves writing and has been writing since she was 10. At first it began with journals and diaries and grew into a passion. She is currently pursuing her masters in film making.

She loves writing, reading and traveling. Her work has been published in various anthologies before. She is an aspiring novelist and wishes to publish her own book soon.

# Solitude.

Raghav wakes up to loud banging on his door. Unsure who it is, Raghav panics and makes his way to the hall downstairs. He grabs a vase in his hand and slowly goes towards the door. The bangs on the door don't stop. Raghav is terrified with no clue what is going on. He quickly shouts, "Who is there? I have a gun, I have called the police, go away", The bangs don't stop. Raghav reaches window near his door and sees a man standing in front of his door with a mask on his face, he tries to recall if he had seen a man like him anywhere but fails to recognize. He hides under the window till the police reaches his place.

Raghav lives alone in his plot which is situated a little far from the town. He knows that even if he shouts nobody will hear him or help him out. Suddenly 10 minutes later the banging sound stops. Raghav decides to wait for the police. Since where he lived is away from the city, it takes 30 minutes for the police to reach to his place. As soon as they reach his place,

they start questioning him about the events. The police take it lightly and tells him not to panic as it could have been a prankster. Somehow Raghav finds it hard to believe because deep down he feels it was more than a prank. He feels as if the way the man banged the door, depicted his anger. The police look in the areas nearby but can't find anyone. Raghav is advised to keep his doors properly locked just for safety. He is asked to call them in case anything happens and is advised to not say anything or move anywhere and be locked up in a safe place in the house so that even If the burglar gets into the house, he can be safe until the police gets there.

The police leaves, Raghav can't sleep. He knows something is very wrong. He stays awake and sits near his window to see if anybody walks up to his house. However, nobody comes.

The next morning Raghav gets ready and leaves for his office without sleeping the whole night. He feels dizzy and wants to sleep but doesn't feel safe at his house anymore. He doesn't tell anyone about what happened and gets straight to work. He decides that he wants to find out what happened so in order to do that he decides to put surveillance camera around his house so anytime anybody walks up he can check the footage on his mobile or laptop. He quickly starts looking for the best cameras online. He checks the reviews and orders them quickly. He thinks of moving to a hotel until then.

After finishing his work, he makes his way to his house and as soon as he reaches his place, he finds a cooler in front of his house. He sees that there are blood stains all over the cooler and on his door bell. He starts panicking and doesn't understand what to do, he quickly calls Shivansh.

Raghu starts yelling and explains shivansh how he isn't safe and explains the whole story. Shivansh doesn't know what to do but asks Raghav to call the police immediately and not touch the cooler and be locked inside his house until they show up. However, Raghav doesn't feel safe and wonders what if this person is inside the house, he runs back to his car and calls the police. Shivansh on the other hand rushes towards Raghav's place so that he can help him out.

The police arrive at his place, Shivansh reaches 15 minutes after the police. Police takes the cooler and starts collecting the DNA from the cooler. They start opening the cooler and find blocks of ice and some body parts inside a plastic zip lock bag. They start collecting the evidence and 33ealize this is more serious than it looks. They immediately send it over to the lab to get the examinations done. The police ask Raghav to immediately vacant the place and move somewhere else as it could be a potential murderer. Raghav informs them that he has ordered a surveillance camera to put around his house which would be installed in the next two days.

Shivansh asks Raghav to stay with him until the police finds out what is going on. Raghav agrees and quickly packs his bags and crashes at Shivansh's place for the next few days.

He finds it difficult to sleep at night knowing there is someone out there to get him. What if he enters the house? What if he goes through my personal belongings? What If he tries to harm someone close to me? Raghav is completely clueless.

Raghav opens his phone and begins typing,

"I think he is back", He hits send to 4 other people.

He buries himself in the pillow, he thinks to himself why would he be back now? After all these years? And if he really is back, he wouldn't let him live in peace. He knows all of them screwed up big time but somehow got away with it. If he is back, he wouldn't be able to live like this for a long time. He would either die or suffocate. He knows who this is but can't say for sure. Suddenly his phone rings, it's the officer leading his case. He asks him to come to the police station immediately. Raghav immediately rushes to the police station.

"All those parts were of different animals. I think somebody is trying to play a dirty prank on you", Says the officer as soon as Raghav sits down to talk.

"How can we find out who is doing this?" He replies.

"We tried to find the DNA but sadly we could only find your matches on the system. There are no fingerprints apart from yours on the door bell and cooler. Which makes me think you might have touched it before we arrived?"

"No I didn't. I don't understand as soon as I saw it I ran back to my car and called you. I think somebody is trying to kill me"

"How can you be so sure about it?"

"Why else would he send body parts to my house? He is trying to indicate something to me"

"Do not panic. We are trying our best to find this person. Please try not to be alone over there until we find something concrete because it is difficult to say what motive this person has",

"Okay, I will do as you say. Thank you for updating me",

Raghav then completes some formalities with the police and heads out. He quickly opens his phone and types another message for the same group, "It is definitely him; He is back. You all need to be safe. If anything comes up, I will inform you all", He sends it to those 4 people again.

Raghav decides to drive back to his place just to have a look. He looks at the clock its 9 pm. He knew the drive would take 30 minutes from the station. He decides to tell Shivansh to go to sleep as he had to talk to the police for some more time and that he would be late. He then rushes to his house to look for evidence or anything that can confirm if he is back. He looks around the house and finds nothing. He starts walking outside the house and starts looking around the backyard, the front porch but doesn't find anything. He finally gives up when he 37ealize37 its 11 pm and decides to drive back. He starts walking up to his car when he finds a moon pendant necklace. He recalls it from those days when he and 4 of his friends screwed up. He starts panicking as he 37ealize37 that he is no longer safe. He has come back to get him. He runs back to his car when he hears footsteps behind him. He runs as fast as he can and gets back in his car and rapidly drives back to the town.

He drives as fast as he can, while driving he can't help his tears from falling. He goes back way into the past and worries about everything that he and his friends did.

## <u>10 Years Ago</u>

Raghav and his friends, Arjun, Gautam, Anna, Aditi and Roma planned a trip to Goa after their finals were over. At first their parents were hesitant but they all somehow convinced their parents and made their way to goa.

Upon reaching Goa they all made plans as to what and how they will explore the city and most importantly what all they will drink. The best part about going out alone was they were able to do things on their own and even drink and party without any restriction.

They headed out to the beach near a shack and sat there and had some drinks. It was not their first time but it was their first time out alone without any restrictions, all of them decided to go crazy and drink like there was no tomorrow.

Raghav decided not to drink much as he wanted to look after the others. Anna on the other hand got hammered like there was no more drinking for her after that night. Arjun and Gautam drank until they could and Aditi and Roma were not into the idea of it. The most fun loving among them all was Anna. Raghav carried Anna to the room where they both fell asleep. Gautam and Arjun

were sharing room, for some reason
Arjun couldn't sleep and hence he
was wandering around the corridor
when he heard Raghav's door open.
It was Anna, "Can't sleep, eh?"
Asked Anna, Arjun politely nodded.
"You know I don't sleep after I
drink, that is one of the most
boring things you can ever do
right?" Arjun replied, "I know
right and look at these idiots as
if we are going to get these days
back, I mean who knows?", They both
were still pretty drunk. Arjun and
Anna continued talking about life,
their goals and plans ahead. It was
getting pretty late and suddenly
Arjun asked Anna, "Why him? Even
when you know how I felt about
you?", "I love him" Replied Anna.
Arjun went quiet. Anna held his
hand and told, "I did feel the same
about you but you never told me and
when you did it was too late",
Arjun nodded and couldn't utter a
single word after that, He asked
Anna to go and sleep. They both
went to their own rooms. Arjun was
heartbroken and didn't know what to
do but he respected their
relationship so decided to stay out

of it. That's the thing about being high you never know how you react to things.

The next morning Anna and Raghav decided to go out alone. They went to a nearby beach and spent some time together. On their way back Raghav decided to buy Anna a necklace. He got her a necklace with a moon's pendant on it. He said she was the moon of his life and he wouldn't let her go ever.

Days passed by and one fine day when all of them were at the beach they saw a man approaching them, He told them that he had different types of drugs available. At first everyone was hesitant but Arjun insisted that they can give it a try, hence he convinced everyone and they ended up buying drugs from that stranger. They all decided to head back to the hotel and give it a try. Anna loved the idea of trying new things and Raghav opposed it. He told Anna not to do it but he couldn't force her so he had to let her do what she wished to do. Arjun and Anna were the only ones who decided to give it a try,

Roma and Aditi didn't support the idea at all so they decided to just head back to their room and sleep. Gautam and Raghav decided to stay back and be with them in case something happens.

Raghav and Gautam eventually fell asleep that's when Anna and Arjun decided to head to another room and play some songs. They went to another room and started doing more drugs. Arjun stopped doing it because he started feeling a little uneasy while on the other hand Anna wasn't ready to stop. Arjun was so high that he fell asleep. Anna kept on partying alone. She was the kind of girl who could get high alone and still be okay with the high and not fall. She fell asleep after sometime.

The next day Raghav asked Anna to never do it again but Anna wanted to do more of it. Anna still promised him that she wouldn't do it again.

However, Anna told Arjun to get more stuff on his way out so that once everyone is asleep, they can do it again. That night after others went to sleep Anna and Arjun decided to do drugs again. This time the drugs felt different. They both were high on different tangent all together. They took breaks between each session. Anna suddenly felt dizzy and she fainted. Arjun thought she has gone to sleep and didn't bother much. He lied down too. It was when he tried waking her and she didn't wake up that he 42ealize42 something was wrong. He ran to other rooms and woke everyone up and told them what exactly happened. Raghav was furious and blamed Arjun for doing this. He told him that he knew how stupid it was and he still decided to do it. However, they all felt that something was seriously wrong. They thought she was dead because of the overdose.

"We need to do something about her, she is not conscious anymore and I don't want us to get in trouble because of the decision that she made." Said Arjun.

"Guys don't listen to him let's just take her to the hospital" Said Raghav.

"Are you serious? What will happen then? We all go to jail because she decided to do so much of it when her body couldn't handle it. I tried to stop her but she didn't she is gone but we have our lives. We can make some story up but first we have to get rid of her body", Arjun tried convincing everybody.

"You have got to be kidding me" Roma said.

"No, I am not" Arjun replied.

Raghav was completely blank and was crying hysterically. He couldn't believe it. He loved her and she was no more. He wished he had just stopped her the day before. He blamed nobody but himself for how things turned out. Aditi tried to console him. Roma agreed with Arjun and so did Gautam. Raghav and Aditi were having a hard time agreeing with Arjun but since the majority won, they couldn't do anything. Arjun told them that if anyone ever opens their mouth, he will make sure that the same person pays for what happened. And they all knew that it was easy to do so.

They all decided to put Anna's body in one big suitcase and find a place to dump it. They went around looking for places first thing in the morning, they came across this river 13 kms away from their hotel which looked abandoned. They decide to go there and dump her body at night. They bought a new big suitcase and took it to the room and put her body in the bag. They hired a car on Gautam's license as he was the only one who was 18 and had a license with him. They all waited for night and as the clock hit 11, they all headed out to the river. They took the suitcase and threw it directly into the river. They then head to the police station at 1 am. They had already decided what to tell the police. "We were sleeping and Anna went missing, we checked everywhere but we can't find her". Raghav was not able to do anything about it. Roma kept on making sure that Raghav stays calm.

They reached the police station and lodged a complaint. All of them gave their statements one by one, everyone tried to portray that Anna wanted to run away and that she wasn't happy. All of their parents were called there and the search began. The police searched everywhere. In the forest, the dumping ground and the police found a suitcase underwater and they found it be suspicious as it looked brand new. They decided to take it outside the river on the sides and check. The suitcase was surprisingly very heavy as well they opened the suitcase and 45ealize it is Anna's body. They quickly held all the kids under their custody and interrogated them but however failed to get any information. They sent Anna's body for autopsy and waited for the results.

When the results came in the police discovered that Anna died because of drug overdose. They didn't release the information and ordered a test on all of them. They went through drug test; everyone cleared but Arjun didn't which raised questions on him. The police tried to interrogate all of them again. Roma 45ealize45 that if Arjun goes down, he will take all of them down with him so she spoke to all of them without Arjun and tried to convince them to testify against Arjun. She told them that all they have to do is tell the police that they both did drugs and we had no idea about it until now. He confessed later. We had no idea about what happened that night because we all slept early. Upon interrogation Raghav told the police that it was Arjun who forced her to do drugs and when things went wrong, he scared all of them by saying he will kill them all too and hence they helped him and did nothing about it. The police filed a case and took Arjun to court. The court decided to sentence Arjun for 3 years without bail as he was under 18 and offered government aid once he was out of the jail.

After the verdict Arjun's parents disowned him; meanwhile the others decided to move far away from Delhi and never keep in touch apart from the time when they feel Arjun is back. Nobody told each other where they went and decided to never share anything with each other. Raghav moved to Kolkata and decided to stay away from the public eye in a secluded area so that even If Arjun returns, he wouldn't be able to get to him.

**Present:-**

Raghav finally reaches his friend's house and runs upstairs. He hides the necklace in the pocket of his jacket and acts as if nothing has happened. He quietly goes inside and goes into his room and locks the room. He starts scrolling through his phone. Tries to find her photo from the day he got her the necklace. He finds it and 47ealize47 how much he misses her, "Anna" He cries himself to sleep.

Raghav looks out the window, its 6 am on a Thursday. He 47ealize47 he is supposed to receive his surveillance camera today. He quickly gets up and gets ready for work, he pretends he is sick and takes half day off and goes back to his house. He asks the technician to install the camera all around the premises and set the app on his phone as well.

After setting it up Raghav moves to Shivansh's place.

Raghav constantly keeps an eye on the monitor so that he knows if someone goes in or comes around his house. But nothing happens. One week passes by but no activity whatsoever. He finally decides to go back to his house, Shivansh tries to stop Raghav from going back because he feels that it is still unsafe for him to go back. Raghav insists and ends up going back.

He goes back cleans up his house and prepares the dinner. He then goes upstairs and tries to go to sleep.

Around midnight at 2 am he hears a car driving near his house and realize48 it is in fact Arjun. This time he walks in with an electric locker and on top of the locker he attaches a paper. Raghav doesn't make any noise and just watches through the CCTV quietly. Arjun looks at the camera and removes his mask and holds a paper which says "You're next". Raghav gets scared. Arjun starts walking back to his

car and drives away. Raghav waits
for a few minutes before finally
going down and see what Arjun left
for him.

He carries the safe into his house
and opens the paper attached to it
he finds a number on it but doesn't
understand what it means. He tries
googling the number and when he
does it gives him a location of a
factory few kms away from his
house. He believes that he is
supposed to be there and finally
ends up deciding to go there. He
gets out and drives into the woods
towards the factory, upon reaching
he discovers that the place is
abandoned. He hesitates but ends up
going inside. He looks around but
doesn't find anything. He walks
towards the centre of the factory
and finds an envelope. He takes the
envelope and drives back to his
house. As soon as he reaches the
house, he opens the envelope, he
finds his photos with Anna from
those days. He goes through each
one of them and as he reaches the
end, he finds that there is a photo
of Anna's dead body which was taken
right after the police found him.

Raghav gets scared and doesn't know what to do. He texts his friend, Gautam, Aditi, Roma to tell them that it is Arjun and he is doing some creepy things to scare him. He tries to get in touch with them but nobody replies. He doesn't understand what exactly happened and he doesn't know where they live so it is impossible for him to find out what exactly is wrong with them. He starts thinking what if Arjun went to them all and killed them.

Raghav constantly tries to get in touch with all of his friends but fails in each attempt. He doesn't understand how Arjun got a hold of his address and found out that he lives here. He tries to open the safe that was left outside the door but is not able to do so. He tries all the possible combinations but the lock just doesn't open.

He continues the normal routine and police check ups he doesn't tell them about Arjun. He wants to know what Arjun wants and he wanted to make sure he was the first person to get in contact with him. Days pass by and he sees Arjun coming by but he doesn't do anything. 4 days into it Arjun stops visiting his house and Raghav feels as if he has gone back.

10 days pass by but nothing happens.

One fine night 10 days after Arjun stops passing by his place, it strikes him that he should try the date when Raghav was convicted. He tries to open the safe and he surprisingly it opens. He finds a letter and it says, "I am going to go away once you tell me why you did what you did. I will be waiting and enjoy the surprise".

He quickly looks inside the safe and finds a plastic bag and along the bag tapes were stuck. It was very difficult for Raghav to open it. He tried feeling the bag and found that whatever was inside was very soft. He thought this could be a part of an animal again. He threw the bag away out of terror. He felt as if it was necessary for him to confront Arjun, that is when his phone rings.

Its his mother. "Arjun, your dad is not doing okay. You need to come back to Delhi as soon as you can. We are at the hospital and they say it doesn't look good", "Maa what happened?", "I don't know it is sudden you have to come here as soon as possible", "Okay Maa, I will be there."

Raghav packs his bags and makes his way to the airport. He calls his office and informs them that he won't be able to attend office for some days because of a family emergency. He buys his ticket and goes to Delhi.

Upon reaching Delhi he straightaway goes to the hospital and looks for his parents. The nurse informs him that there is nobody who is admitted under his father's name. He feels as if something is definitely wrong. He runs outside the hospital and rushes to his house. As he walks in, he feels as if no one is in there. He searches every room and every floor of the house but no one is at home. He hears a vehicle coming into his garage. He rushes down to see who it is and finds it to be Arjun.

"Welcome back buddy, Remember me?" Says Arjun.

"What do you want?" Raghav murmurs

"I just wanted to see you, Is it so bad?"

"You need to leave right now or I will call the police"

"Go ahead, give it a try and see if they pick up" Says Arjun and starts laughing hysterically.

"What do you want me to do? Where are my parents?"

"Oh they? They are safe somewhere away from here" He walks towards Raghav and hands him a phone. As Raghav looks at the phone he 53ealize53 it is his mother's phone. This makes Raghav very angry and he holds Arjun by his collar and yells, "Where is my mother? What have you done? What is wrong with you?", Arjun slowly moves Raghav's hand away from his collar and says, "Patience, They are fine but before I release them I want you to surrender to the police and tell them what lies you told", "You know that is not possible" Raghav replies.

"Well It is if you try", Says Arjun

"I will do it, first tell me where my parents are and I want to speak to them"

"Alright Alright. I will let you speak to them."

Arjun removes a burner phone and dials a number, "Hello, pass the phone to her now" He then gives the phone to Raghav,

"Hello maa, are you okay??" Raghav asks

"Be—Betaa Please be safe. We are ---" and the voice goes silent.

"What the hell. I need you to release her right now and I will do as you say" Raghav tells Arjun while smashing the phone to the ground.

"Slowly, I don't have the luxury of buying phones like you. It was really difficult for me to even get this one. While all of you got good bloody jobs. I was stuck in Jail and then stuck at some gas station not being able to find a good job" He continues while folding his sleeves, "You know how it is for me? My parents won't look me in the face. I didn't do anything wrong. You all were equally involved. If you really wanted to do something you would have done it in that moment but you didn't which makes you as terrible as I am",

"Look its in the past, you want money. Take money, Hell take this house stay here I will pay the bills but you have to leave my parents. Me telling the police won't do them any good."

"Don't you dare negotiate. Tonight, I will kill your parents and then you will know how it feels to lose someone and be assured that you will be held responsible for it"

"I lost her you know I lost something too.."

Arjun interrupts Raghav, "You can never compare it to things that I lost. I lost my family, my career, my reputation and mostly my dreams."

"Look I will help you" Raghav gets on his knees and begs Arjun to leave his parents. But Arjun doesn't listen to him. He then removes a gun and tells Raghav to be quiet and tells him to go and sit on a chair. He ties Raghav to a chair and doesn't let him move. He then takes another chair and sits right in front of Raghav and uses Raghav's phone to call the same guy he called before and mutters, "Kill them", Upon hearing this Raghav goes numb and he yells on the top of his voice no, no, no. But then Arjun puts the phone on speaker and they hear 4 gunshots and screaming voice of his parents. As Raghav hears this he breaks down completely into tears. Meanwhile, Arjun laughs standing there and looks at Raghav fiercely and asks him how it feels, to which he doesn't reply.

Arjun finally after 10 minutes walks up to Raghav, He calls the man again and puts it on speaker, "Arey beta you came back, you didn't tell me. Don't worry me and baba came out to buy some groceries we will be back in another hour.

Let me know if you want to eat something", Raghav looks up and doesn't understand what is exactly happening. Arjun disconnects the call and says, "I never killed them. All that you heard was a mix of recording and I wanted to make you feel how I felt. I can't even see my parents. Hell, I can't live well. I struggle to eat food because of what you guys did to me. I thought you wouldn't do anything against me but you were the one to tell the police that it was all my idea. I wanted to make you feel the pain and I am successful in doing so. Your parents are safe, nothing has happened to them. You can call them. Roma, Aditi and Gautam are safe. I just made sure they didn't receive your message. You guys can keep your friendship alive. No matter what I will never ever do anything to harm you because I am not the monster, you are." He throws the phone towards Raghav and walks away.

Raghav 57ealize57 how selfish he and his friends had been. He understands how they all spoiled his life and saved themselves. He couldn't believe the monster he had become up until now. He was working at a good company living his dream. He kept on thinking how Arjun must feel now that he has nothing with him. He wanted to apologise but didn't know how to.

This incident completely changed Raghav. He finally moved back to Delhi and lived with his parents. He started visiting Arjun every now and then but didn't have the guts to speak to him. He just looked at how

he was doing and if ever needed he tried to help him out. He also tried to keep in touch with Anna's family knowing she was the only daughter they had. His outlook on life changed and made him 58ealize how blessed he really was all along.

# Ishani Bali

Instagram Id: num_in_ous

Ishani Bali
pursuing physiotherapy
Age 20

Admin of – num_in_ous.
started writing at the age of 16
favourite author – John Green.

If I get lost somewhere in this
perilous universe,


Will you come in search of me?
When I will be missing,


Will my absence bother you?
If I become a past memory,
will you remember my love forever?

**★★★★**

I don't know what are we but you
are the answers to all my
questions, reason my soul feels so
alive, my heart skips a beat,
missing piece of my heart, blush at
random thoughts.

Little did I know this is called
love.
Little do I know if you feel the
same.


**★★★★**

Trust is a thin thread woven with
your gestures and words don't let
it break by unwanted Vibrations of
mistrust.

****

It's good to sort things and
forget,
It's good to stay calm when
betrayed,
It's good to forgive when taken for
granted,
It's good to be a kind heart in
this cruel world.

****

Even though orchid is associated
with virility,
it represents the characteristics
of a strong woman -
A beauty, elegance, love, delicate,
strength.

****

Never make any  perpetual
perspective towards someone,
 It can either kill them or kill
you with infamy.

****

He messed up and apologized she
quoted 'LOVE IS NOT GUILT, LOVE IS
TRUST.'

****

Musical waves under the bright
night sky, dancing on the rock on
the melody of the waves, arms
wrapped around each other.  he
whispered I found the one - you're
the one all I want.' she looked him
in the eye and replied 'forever'.
kissed her forehead, 'perfect'
acknowledged together.

********

My mind is wrapped around you that
is the reason I sense your presence
even when you are not next to me.

********

You are unicorn to my rainbow.

********

****

Threw his bag on the floor.
Dumped himself on the bed.
Lights off
Thinking caps on.
What is wrong with me?
Am I abnormal?
Am I suffering from a mental
disorder?
I love him, what to do?
Can mom and dad accept that I have
feelings for a guy?
 I have accepted my self, why isn't
the society ?
This puzzle traps me and my
identity in the chains of rules of
the society.

Girl loves boy - Wow!
Boy loves Girl- Wow!
Boy loves boy - Oh no!
Girl loves Girl - Ewww!

In the end his innocent soul
succumbed to the guidelines of the
society.
One more love story died before it
could even flourish..

****

****

"Oculus reparo", she waved the
broken branch.
"You're not Hermione Granger!", he
exclaimed.

****


Heart : Is there somebody who can
help me?
I need somebody now !!

Brain : oh-god not again ! it's
time for another shot of espresso.

****

Never refuse to help anyone in
need,
Remember Karma is requital, won't
spare you.

****

****

I still remember our first
conversation.
we knew this was special and
decided to be each other's night
chills and morning warmth.


Long drives listening to our
favourite songs that described our
crazy bond are unforgettable.

Little did we know about the
thunderstorms and the rain.

Little did I know that I was giving
it more than I should have.

You shattered me into pieces and
one with love remained unfound
still.

I just wish happiness finds you
where ever you are and get what you
deserve.
You will be my special forever but
not by my side.


****

********

Took her first time in his arms ,
Eyes filled with happy tears,
My princess 'was his first words
after seeing her mesmerizing eyes.

Helped her walk her first steps,
Protected her from nightmare demons
by his lullaby's, She slept with a
smile.
After six  months three days she
finally said her first word pa- pa,
that day he was the most happiest
person on this planet.

He stood behind her like a pillar,
Helped her get through every
situation,
All her mistakes were corrected by
him.

All his hard work paid off,
As she was awarded  world best
doctor,
She quoted 'all because of my
Paa '.
Second time his eyes filled with
happy tears.
Proved as always,
Father daughter relation is more
precious than a white Pearl.

# Lisha Desale

Instagram Id:lisha__suryawanshi

A lusty Bibliophile. A human who believes in sniffing books, enjoying coffee on a sleepy night to top off the journey lying in hands, and words of wisdom in mind.

One who sleeps with books on bed, books in closet, but not in shelf. One who won't stick to genres but explore through every letter.

# Fond Mothers, Dr. Strange and a Loving Partner.

I ended up confessing my mother about the love of my life. My heart was warning me burglarously. I was asking myself: do you have any guesses about the end? Any guesses about the reaction of mother? Any guesses about the conclusion? Conclusion! Umm... Not so good. It was bitter sweet. Bitter from her side. And sweet, well sweet from none. It was constantly poking me to not take that action. Back to that time, I don't remember whether "it" was my mind or my heart. The whole confession scene was like stabbing into my own back. That episode did not go well. Not at all. She ended up getting angry with me. This was bound to happen, I was not ready for it. It was an action taken thoughtlessly, without considering all the possibilities. Possibilities; this word in this era reminds me of one grandeur; Avengers and Dr. Strange! I wish I had time stone to check all the possibilities over this situation. But to no avail, a no from a mother is a no! And like a small child I cried for my favourite chocolate. I argued, I panicked, I tried convincing her. Well on that note, my partner told me that my behaviour and efforts were no where close to the word "convincing". Sad. I was all over the place getting chaotic in the house while trying to talk about this love situation to my mother around eleven o' clock at night, when she was about to go to bed after a tiresome day. Woah! Mistakes: one after the other. Well I give him the point, for who knows me better than the both of them now. And I did not take this love confession scenario so seriously after that night. Because my mother knows she has a stubborn daughter with a very good choice and a good taste. So she knows the future. Even if the present is a big no for all that I wanted. What I wanted? I wanted her to meet him formally as someone her daughter has chosen for lifetime. Well if not now, but some years later, that will definitely happen;

a formal meeting!
My mother is a beautiful
photographer, not a professional
one, but a proud one. She is a
proud mother to a daughter she
brought up and pampered. So she has
always loved taking my photographs,
candid ones to be specific and also
the ones where she would set the
outfit, a bit of plating and
folding the ethnics one, a bit of
elegant touch. Trust me she has
clicked the best candid ones for me
and I post those on social media
too. Now you must have understood
the level of beauty. Sheer one.
About me here, I have been an
impatient model, making stupid
faces and ignoring my mother's
photography skills. I am a pathetic
model. And thank good we both know
that. Otherwise she would have
ended up sending me into some
modelling assignments. Modelling
assignments and my partner's
mother, a sweet lady she is. She
had asked me to participate in one
of those. Can you believe it! I am
dealing with too much sweetness in
my life, sweetness showering from
the best of both the worlds. But I

was never interested in that path. So anyway I ended up hiring a personal photographer, like you can see. And to my luck, both of my ladies are very fond of me. What else one needs in life! Just being thankful. Touchwood. I hope everyone is appreciating these wonderful people around them and the blissful things they do for us.

Wonderful people of my life includes this wonderful person too! That's him, my loving partner. Well we had no common grounds, yet here we are today, together. He knows about the confession scenario. He was a little upset but he said few amazing words, and those words made me have jiggles in my belly. "Never forget, no matter what, for both of us; me and your mother, you will always be our only choice, we live for you". He said it doesn't matter what this life will bring down to our aisle, we would come back to you alone, our only choice, our only conclusion, the only thing that matters to both of us.

That being the world to me, and

that's all about my super awesome
humans. Three cheers to this
beautiful world they create for us!

# Anger and patience : She gave me the best.

Two of the most important things to keep in life; patience and self belief, I had one; self belief. Talking about patience, for me it was quite a task to inculcate. It is still a task to absorb in. I am this strong headed, over ambitious, nerdy suburban young woman, bought up in a very sophisticated zone, struggling hard to be patient. Oh! Well right, sophistication should have bought patience too. But no, did not happen to me. I always thought, me being impatient was my parenting fault. I was a pampered yet responsible kid in the house. My mother being a single parent did the best she could to give me a life better than anyone could have asked for through the situations we outgrew. Life it is. We learn to deal with it. So being pampered in a certain context, my anger got pampered too. My point is; it is good to have a strong head. It is good to be impatient. We all grew to this age today following different paths to Pave the way for this life. We learned a million things knowingly and unknowingly. We hold a certain set of qualities. We hold a certain set of ethics and beliefs. We learn each and every day, we learn every moment. So it's alright to have certain qualities. Good or bad. Everyone has it. So it's alright to have a short temper. It has helped me stay strong over the years, saved me through various disastrous events. It gave me strength. It made me ambitious, probably over ambitious! It made me hold and blunt. It made audacious and capable. Occasionally, makes me little dominant and manipulative. I am all proud about it. Also, being impatient and having anger issues in certain situations is a very wicked thing to have. It can hurt others. Especially people you love and who love you back. We drain our emotions out on them. We take them for granted and pour out unwanted feelings and burdens on them in various forms. No one is proud about it. Me neither, and I still haven't mastered the art to controlling my anger. I am Learning. Have I been shy and calm, it would have helped me in different way. But somewhere it feels that the world would have been dominant and manipulative. Well, there are two sides to a coin; two sides to a quality too. So, today I am happy about my qualities, for what they have made me, for this life the way it has been, for the way it will be. My mother did not fail anywhere and I am no one to blame her for anything. These are the best qualities she formed me with. We all have grown into beautiful people, we are responsible and mature enough to make our choices and anything good or bad within us, about us; we should be taking responsibilities for that. We all have our share of scars, but one needs to live with that and above. Hope we all make the most of our qualities and learn to be the Masters.

# Today, it happened for three times!

1st he got angry about an amalgamated statement. I somehow calmed him down and he did calm down by himself. Anger gets triggered because I speak in an unfinished, equivocal pattern. Somewhere it's true. But he was as usual inquisitive, went on asking questions, I tried answering one after the other, ambiguously. I was so busy typing hurriedly in between the lecture, that I forgot I was speaking in uncertainty. Somehow that anger passed us by. A few words spilled in, to sound harsh. But we managed. That's the skill; to manage, to let go, may be to ignore too.

For the second time he got angry was in the afternoon; it was because I missed his calls, two calls. One on WhatsApp and another a normal one. I left my phone in the car and I was busy washing the car. My negligence caused him trigger his anger. I ended up disconnecting his third call, a

video call; because my mother was
around. Here I did manage to calm
him down.

The third was at night, when it
seemed he was uninterested to talk
and I went out of topics. I was
drained emotionally. Nothing
serious happened, but I felt
enervated. I thought may be I
should sleep. So I told him I am
going to bed; I have nothing else
to do. But he seemed to be
expecting something else: a good
night and a love you may be. Or
anything else other than those
heart emojis which weren't
sufficient to suppress his anger.
Well few messages preceded by, I
did say I love you infinitely baby,
good night. But forgot to say so in
the later part. Eventually he got
furious. I tried to calm him down,
I tried to keep myself patient
enough to gulp his anger and to be
a pacifier. But I cried while
trying to lord over.
It's hard to calm him, his temper
and his aggression. It's hard to
understand him. But I am trying.
Also I have to take care of the

"me" I have, by keeping myself intact. I know I will make it through. I know that one day things will be jovial. I know that this is just a phase and it will pass. I know that he is not able to give his 100 percent because of the path he is fighting through. He is trying too; trying hard to stay, trying hard to keep me, trying hard to dust off the sufferings, trying hard to be happy, trying hard to give us that 100 percent we deserve. I know that every second of the clock, he is suffering through immense pain, and it's hard to understand the depth of his scars: for he who suffer knows his suffering better than the breath of one's life. If there was a chance, I would happily share his sorrow, his sickness, his proliferating problems. But all I can do is stay, and stay calm. Wait and be patient; for I have a strong head and I am being tested too. So I have to stay and Keep him at peace and that being for the rest of my life too. At the end all that we have is our share of sufferings. When it's time to put out our best, one should definitely do so without giving a second thought, even if it feels draining. Even if it feels that too much of you is being demanded, too much of you is taken away, you should give. Had it not been you and the abundance you hold, the situations would have never struck you. So it's alright to give your hundred percent on days when people around you, who matter to you are unable to give cent percent. Time revolves and it is the key.

# Roses.

Yes! He brought me roses - a bouquet of roses to be specific, Scarlet orange; bright and beaming. Well, these being my favourite shades to play with; scarlets and oranges and reds and yellows always made me gleam in their tones. He came and sat in the car, I couldn't believe the romantic gesture he had shown. I was flabbergasted by looking at those flowers, his efforts, his love, I was amazed to look at him. Without delaying I took the roses from him, sniffed those, felt them, felt the rosy fragrance, felt the icy jitter and freshness they brought me in those moments. I sat there holding them for a long time, feeling felicitous. It was not about the roses alone, but the feeling that I was special, the feeling that all those efforts were taken for me, the feeling that he knew little things mattered the most, these authentic gestures were important to me and he knew it. Out of all the errands he had to entertain, he chose to bring me smiles! He chose to make memories, he chose me!

Out of all the chaos happening in one's life, they get you flowers, they get you kisses, warm soothing hugs, ravishing support, tremendous help and sometimes a pile of responsibilities too; all you can do is appreciate it. Enjoy it and love every bit of it. They take out some time just to bother you to relive those moments they spent processing and adapting to the thoughts, right from buying the flowers to delivering it to you, just to see a smile on your face. Not just the flowers but every bit these people do for you, every step they take towards you, matters! We should be appreciative as well as wise enough to bring back the same for them. Making a journey of miles and crossing all other worries off, they come to you, that's more than enough for your world spearing down an axe in this world of reality, trying to prove and make a

place for your love and your world. That's more than enough, those people taking efforts for you are

enough for you and so are you for
yourself and for them. Keep them,
keep those flowers, keep those
moments, keep everything that
brings a smile on your face and
love in your life. Keep the
authenticity of a bond, do not ever
term it to be materialistic, do not
make that mistake ever.

# Mritika Mazumder

Instagram Id: m2_poemwritter

My name is Mritika Mazumder, a unique name with a unique personality. I am a poet, sort of writer who love to engage with different generation's by writing skills. I believe that words can catch the emotions once it can be felt and penned down on a paper.

You will love my collection of writings and can read it on my insta handle m2_poemwritter.

# The sexiest thing about smoking.

Smoking is injurious to health written on every packet of a cigarette whether it is of any cost but do the people who smoke really quit reading the same? No, I think they quit reading that line.
To all the smoker in the group cheers to all and a puff because I am writing about the sexiest thing about smoking.First day, a guy took a cigarette in his hand thought his parents will be going to kill him but the supportive friends encouraged him and he took a puff of it. Yes, he coughed a little but he felt the coolest among in the group. This is the sexiest thing about smoking is.
A round table, puff of cigarette and a sip of tea made a perfect combo. The line "chal sutta pike aate hai" has a unique feeling.

The street corner stall, the unknown people meeting for the first time asking for a lighter

made them close, yes why not
smoking is sexiest thing.
A dude in the group, rings in the
air and all clap why not smoking is
sexiest.
One cigarette divided in 12 and a
strong bond just a puff made them a
family why not smoking is sexy
thing.A girl smoking with her guy
friend became a charm in the group
and she always have someone with
her who always cares her why not
smoking is sexiest. He was upset,
he went to the street corner and
again meet the same person to share
all the feelings with a puff of
cigarette, he got a life time
friend why not smoking is sexiest.
Yes he had a cancer because of
smoking but he has his friends on
his side whom he got while smoking
why not smoking is sexiest.
Yes smoking is dangerous, people
should quit it after a stage but
looking a person smoke feels him
like smoking is sexiest. Smoking is
sexiest thing, it makes environment
pollute but people who smoke plant
trees too.

# Two shots of whiskey fall in love with five shots of vodka

Brown liquor in his hand, white
liquor in her
Looking each other in eyes lock
It made a shot of whiskey fall in
love with five shots of vodka
Songs on high beat, getting closer
to each other
Hand in hand, dancing together,
He ordered another shot of whiskey
and a shot of vodka to made them
fall in love with each other.
She started to drink one after
other, stopped at five, legs
shaking but he made her comfortable
that's how two shots of whiskey
fall in love with five shots of
vodka.
She drank for the first time but he
was used to it
She danced like a mad in the crowd;
Taking him round and round that's
how two shots of whiskey fall in
love with five shots of vodka.
She trusted him and he didn't broke
it. She tries to hung up, tries to
kiss him. But he controlled her and
that day

Five shots of vodka made her fall
in love with two shots of whiskey.
Hand in hand after a year, they
both took one shot of whiskey
Memorizing that day when they fall
in love with each other
Thanks that two shots of whiskey
and five shots of vodka that made
them fall in love with each other.

# Gender discrimination

I'm born in a country
Where equality is my right,
But not followed
Why people say I'm a girl not a boy
Just because I have my monthly
period and a boy doesn't
Or I gave birth to a generation and
what a boy can't do
Why a boy can stalk a girl and no
one says a word?
Why not a girl can stalk a boy?
Yes I saw a case where a girl gets
a reserved seats and boy doesn't
Yes I saw a man talking about
having a baby boy not a girl
My heart skipped a beat and pain
got fill in it
Yes I'm a girl and I'm against
gender discrimination
I want everyone to be treated
equally
Because I'm born in a country
Where equality is my right.

# Fate of our love

Seeing you through the balcony was
my favourite pass time,
Our heart beats when our eyes
caught together,
Seeing each other and a shy smile.
I like the way you tried talking to
me,
I like the way you smile when you
see me,
I still remember the first
handshake with you,
But our destiny is not what we
thought.
Our small conversation, your one
high volume note,
Made my heart felt bad,
Yes I broke down that day when you
slapped me
And that's the fate of our love
We can't be together forever.

Can we be friends again?

I just wanted to say something,
I wish you can give me a chance,
I always sees your status
You are so happy and I wanted you
to be.
Sometimes I really wanted to say "

I Miss you" can we be friends again
but I can't,
I wish you could give me a chance
to talk,
I wish we can clear our
misunderstandings,
I wish we can be a roommate again,
I wish I can again take your shoes
and wear it again,
I wish we could be friends again,
But I know I can just wish,
As every wish doesn't come true
But I know I fine day you will be
there to talk to me and I promise I
will not be there to reply
you......

# Nishita M. Agath

Instagram ID: nishita_agath

BELIEVER, Because I believe someday stars
will shine & fireflies will glow,

Writing is my kind of meditation,

Doer over thinker,

Less of ambitious & more of a dreamer,

Employed by my own bubble of imaginations,

Craziness runs in my blood & obsessed with
being happy.!

They decided to meet again, they talked, they tried to sort out everything, They began it in the same way as it all started, Yes they gave one more chance to their relationship.!  & Sometimes Ego loses & love wins.

"Look another entertaining thing have started there. One more lust story has begun in the class.!" classmates exclaimed. Few years later, their wedding card reflected it was LOVE & not the lust.!

Dear love, From playing hide & seek to hiding tears & always seeking each other's happiness, From sharing chocolates to sharing secrets, From being friends to watching F.R.I.E.N.D.S, From best friend to soulmate, From writing names on last pages of books to having names on wedding card,  From You and Me to Us, I feel extraordinarily blessed to have this forever kinda thing.!

~ yours childhood love.!

****

From being my happiness to the one I'll never want to remember, From being my reason to smile to the reason I shed hundreds of tears, From ignoring everyone else just to talk to you to talking to all just to ignore you, From blushing as and when I hear your name to trying so hard even not to think of you, From you being my most favourite person to you being the only one whom I hate even to talk about, LOVE FADED.!

It's not always about who you look best with, But its about with whom you can be Simply YOURSELF.

In the world full of smooth spoken mouths and fake masks, what made me fall for him was his plain spoken & honest nature.

**★★★★**

Dear Kabir Singh,

You are now the one whom I look for
in my love, The one who showed
forever is surely a long
& challenging way but isn't an
impossible thing, the one who loved
at first sight & managed to be
committed till the last breathe,
The one who no matter what didn't
stop loving his girl in any of the
circumstances, the one who
destroyed self just for the one
whom he loved so hard,  From
calling her "YOURS" since the day
you saw to proudly saying her
"YOURS BANDI" even after
separation. Thank you for setting
marvellous relationship
goals.  From protecting her to
standing with her at every step,
From not letting love spoil the car
eer to loving her throughout the
journey, You showed how mutual
efforts works. YOU LOVE THE WAY SHE
BREATHES & I LOVED THE WAY YOU
LOVED.

Yours truly, Fan forever.!

**** 

Its okay if he wasn't able to talk with you the whole day, its

Okay if someday he can't deal with your mood swings, its

Okay if he wasn't able to fulfill what he promised
earlier, it's okay if sometimes he prioritize his goals instead of you, Yes it's okay because he might be imperfect but his love will surely be perfect.!

**★★★★**

"I love you to the moon & back", her fiancé smirked cheerily, "You might be showering love upon her as a princess, but I have loved her & will always do so in her Anabelle version too" Best friend sighed.!

**★★★★**

As irritating as jerry to tom As helpful as motu to patlu, As understanding as oswald to wini, As loving as mickey to minnie, As protective as oggy to jack, As forever bonding as  doreamon & nobita! Yes! Some relations are

simply more than just a
relationship.!

********

His peace : spending time with her

His dreams : fulfill her every wish

His comfort : her nonsense talks

His home : filled with her loud
laughs & cherished memories

His world : her girl As father is
daughter's first love likewise A
daughter is father's LIFE .!

********

Dear Love,

You made me feel the way I can't
even imagine, you have Gifted me
with the memories I can't describe,
you have filled the happiness
beneath me I can't be enough
thankful for. Knowing my weaknesses
you managed to be my strength,
Erasing the dark days writen by
destiny is in no one's hand, but
you are the one who walked with me
during those days and enlightened
my life, Thankyou for Accepting me
the way I am, loving me with all my
negativities and handling my ever
changing mood swings. I love you
with all my heart, because you are
the one who makes my life a little
more happier, crazier, and worth
living.

**★★★★**

"I love you" "I love you too" Love
surely faded between them but
gallery holded on
their love in the form of
screenshots.!

**★★★★**

A child is always god's gift
Somewhere he fills the happiness in
the entire home,  While somewhere
he fills the pockets & helps to
feed the entire home!

****

IDon't want any perfect mate for my
soul, but just the one who fits in
as a jigsaw puzzle's missing part &
fixes all my life's indifferences
till eternity.

****

Gallery: The only place other than
my heart which was owned by HIM.

1 picture - thousands of memories 1
message - millions of smiles 1 call
- tonnes of laughters 1 meeting -
Infinite Happiness 1 person -
Lifeline Cheers to this kind of
blissful Bond.

****

From calling her as her mom's
daughter to calling her as mine
daughter's mom, the most blissful
thing called love happened.

****

"He isn't perfect for you, You will definitely find someone better then him", They said "He might not be perfect for me, But will love me perfectly with all his imperfections. I don't want any better one, I have already got mine best." She proudly replied.

********

Instead of expensive gifts, surprises and celebrations, A simple handwritten diary full of love, feelings & memories created together from the special person makes the birthday marvellous & much more special.

********

I never believed that forever exists, And then he came in my life, the one who never said I will be your forever, But proved with every little thing, in every possible way, on every day along with love, care & utmost respect. Yes some people really proves out to be a blessing we will always be thankful for.

********

Hangover: His smile still shining before my eyes, his voice still on my ears, his laughter still on my head, even after few days of our outing.

Luck: Billions of people in this world and I got him

Love: Hundreds and thousands promises made by people all around and I got someone who proves it in every way without even letting me know

Life: No regrets, no complaints, rather Grateful & blessed to be able to live this life with him.

**LOVE:** "I LOVE YOU" uttered by boyfriend thousands of times proved wrong every time with utmost support & infinite love by BESTFRIEND.

"What do you want to be in future?" They asked. "To be Hers", He replied.

My bucket list:  Wish to become independent, Travel the entire world solely, Getting tattoo inked, To have weekend outings, Be a child even in an adulthood, Hundreds of

wishes, Thousands of dreams,
Rejected by entire home,  Accepted
by one, MY DAD has always proven
being a superhero without any wings
& superpowers.

★★★★

# Saramitra

102

Instagram Id: poet_by_soul__

Hi! I am Saramitra. Currently doing my BE CSE at C I T. My hobbies are reading and writing.

I'm also an amateur freelance graphics designer.

# Escapade

Hate counsels my mind,
I cannot escape.
Depression knocks on my door,
I cannot escape.
Sadness comes to my life,
I cannot escape.
Fear tears me down,
Yet I cannot escape.
But I have a hope in my heart,
A will power to live,
Live, live and live forever.
I will stand on it.
And surely one day I will escape,
Escape, escape and escape.
From that darkness and gloom of my
life,
That now exists as a dark cloud,
Over all my happiness and joys.
I will live till I escape,
And when I escape, I will become
free…

# I Set You Free

Go. Go as far as you can,
As free as a free bird,
As high as the eagle,
And as deep as the oceans.

Go. Go touch the skies,
Float with the clouds,
And play with the cosmos.

Because I have set you free.
Free from all the clutches of life
and death,
From all the pains and sorrows,
And free from all the cages that
may ever hold you here.

********

I feel blessed and highly favoured
when I realise that in this
inhumane world, I could find
someone as humane as you.

********

# What Gives You The Right?

What gives you the right,
To leave me when I need you?
If you entered my life only to
leave,
Then why did you promise me dear,
That you'll never ever leave me?

What gives you the right,
To give me hurt rather than
comfort,
When you told me otherwise?
You said you never ever meant to
hurt me,
But then why your eyes speak its a
lie?.
What gives you the right,
To crack me when I fall?
If you only wanted me to shatter,
Then why did you fake me dear,
That you would always be my healer?
Tell me why? Oh dear,
Please tell me why?
If all you wanted was hate and
rage,
Then why did you shower me,
With all your lies and fears?

# To Be You!

In this world of make-believe's,
Where you can be anyone in this
world,
Choose to be the real You.
You are not Broken nor Lost,
Because you are a great Soul.

And never forget no matter what,
You are Beautiful.
Don't take it to your heart when
Someone says you otherwise.
Your abilities are far more than
worthy to be compared.
And you are the one who decides
Don't follow the crowd.
Separate apart and find where you
stand.
Standing your own ground is the
best thing in this world.
Because no one can steal it from
you, no matter what.
At last, don't forget to live the
moment.
Redefine what is possible,
Live your dreams to the fullest.
Because that is the sole purpose of
Life.

# My Master

Up or down, you are always there,
Side by side you walk
With me aware or unaware
I may complain or thank,
But you are always there to listen,
When nobody is there.
With each step I take, there are
two step of yours,
And with each passing day, you draw
me to you near.
I should be foolish to resist your
call
For you turn my life pure.
You took away people from my life
for a cause,
It would be stupid of me,
To call back on them even for a
pause.
The loved ones of my life
Who left earth and reached your
heaven's doors,
With me here singing their lament
chords.
It wouldn't be great of me to call
back
On those who have reached your
doors,
For you are sure great and make

them shear.
And when I reach the end,
I'll thank you with all the grace,
To help me each and everywhere,
For you are My Master, My Grave!

# Breathe!

Breathe, breathe, breathe!
Because you have got every right
to.
Live, live, live!
Because you have got every right
to.
Stand, stand, stand!
Because no one can pull your legs
down or cut them.
Dream, dream, dream!
Because no one can decide for you
and you don't live for them.
Realize, Realize, Realize!
Because a dark, half-awakened mind
will not lead you anywhere.
Think, think, think!
Because that's where your real
power blooms to everywhere.
Learn, learn, learn!
Because that's how you can change
the world.
Love, love, love!
Because that's the only perfect
gift of this imperfect world.
But never forget to breathe,
because that's your only gift that
cannot be stolen from you.
And never forget to smile, because

that's how the world will be
changed by you.
And in closing, never live for
others, because your life only
belongs to YOU.

# PAIN

Your wild thoughts break my heart
Words strewn across the table
That laps me up in a grievous storm
Shredding me inside a vicious dorm
My heart, my soul-
And oh, there goes my being into it
Until I become nought.
But still the storm brews
Engulfing, shredding and piercing
And yet there remains one:
P-A-I-N
The word that makes me hollow
The thing that eats me out
Leaving anything but a large hole
Until I become just invisible
And I feel anything but numb
Ah, there's my pleasure,
The art of becoming invisible.

# A Bloody Roar

The drums start rolling
And the bells start to ring
Sky blue turns to grey
And I think it's twilight
tik-tok, tik-tok
The time was running down
Darkness just entwines around
And the devils have bloomed.
All were awaiting the final call
Of Death. Of Life. Of Faith.
Storm blows around everywhere
And even hopes shatter here and
there
Until there becomes nothing but
rage
Anything but a cage
People dance in ecstasy
Anticipating the unique fall
When the rain finally starts to
pour
Its nothing but a bloody roar.

# True Friends

Life is a journey as we all know,
Like a train, people do come and
go.
Some for a season, Some for a
reason,
Some might not even care,
But some may become friends
Yet they may forget move away or
just change,
Yet in this inhumane world,
There is someone, whom you can
truly call yours,
Pillar of support and Path to
success,
Holds your hands through
vicissitudes of forever.
True friends with true love,
Hard to find, difficult to leave,
and impossible to forget,
So real and so true friend I have
found,
The only person have I till
forever,
Is You.

# Sunit Agarwal

Instagram Id: the_ugly_words

I'm Sunit Agarwal
From Pakyong, Sikkim, India.

My hobbies are writing,

drawing and cooking.

Admin of ink_that_never_fades.
A businessman at 21.

Tring! Tring!
- Yes, who's there?
- it's love at your door steps
ma'am.
- Go away, I don't need love.
- why?
- I'm already broken.
- Trust me ma'am, the love I'll
give is absolutely immortal.
- Wait, how do I trust you?
- You can return me love when you

****

I can show "How YOU ARE",
But I can't show you, "WHAT YOU
ARE" a mirror said.

****

In this era of "TECHNOLOGY" no once
can be cheated, people have become
"SMART"
Love failures continues..
Where's your technology?
Where's your smartness?

# An open letter to my best friend.

Dear Friend,

I hope you're fine, I'm fine enough to sustain. I know you may be surprised as in the era of Messenger, Facebook, Skype, Twitter, Instagram, Snapchat, WhatsApp and Hike, I'm writing a letter to you. Just saw your new profile picture on Facebook, you're looking cute with her. I'm writing this letter to you just to compliment you on your new happy life as there wasn't any reply from you on any of the social sites. Ok I understand you need to give your time to your valuable friends. But calling these new so called social sites as social does really make a sense? You share a Meme everyday on Facebook, You maintain snap streak, You retweet your favourite star, You share a boomerang everyday on Insta, You share a story on WhatsApp, You just show stickers on Hike and You Never make a call. Oh you feel we're connected. I do feel we are connected yet so disconnected.

I hope you take some of your valuable time to reply this old fashioned system of letter. I can understand you're busy with you life, hence, expectations are least.

Your Always

Golu.

# HUMANITY

I was walking off the street, it was bright, sunny and just an amazing day until I saw a butcher, butchering a cow, without mercy, I could feel the tears in eyes of that innocent animal, wish if only those tears could speak the humanity would have spoken, I lost the faith in humanity. Humanity lose when people win.

Just then, a dog who was crossing the road was about to get hit by a car which was running over-speed, all of a sudden a boy may be around 10 jumped from nowhere and saved the life of a dog, I was just about to gain my faith in humanity unless I saw the boy lying on the road got hit by the car that has already flown away, and the most difficult part was the crowd had already surrounded the boy with their smartphones in hand. I just peeked at one of those, and what I saw, after that humanity cried. I lost the hope in humanity. While every one was busy watching the boy, the dog he saved ran towards the

hospital and called the doctor.
Went home and logged into Facebook,
and there was 10k likes and 8k
comments on the post that person
made *"BRAVE BOY SAVED A DOG'S LIFE
SACRIFICING HIS"* while the boy was
still breathing heavily.
People killed Humanity. I'm afraid
animals don't kill animality.

****

Searching For;
For the truth in the lies,
For love in the hate,
For priority in the anteriority,
For worth in worthlessness,
For beliefs in disbelief,
For honesty in dishonesty,
For trust in mistrust and;
For entity in nonentity,
Somehow you lost your SELF RESPECT.

****

Walking with a 100k smart phone in
hand and with eyes on the screen, A
man bumped with a beggar along
side.

Me: I'm sor...
Ego: Hey? Hey? Hey? Wait!
Me: What?
Ego: Look at him and look at you,
think of where will your status
drop if you ask him sorry.
Me: Oh you're right.

Hey, can't you see a man walking?
You idiot, you made my clothes
dirty. Oh, I need to buy new set of
clothes.

Ego won! But, for me the status of
man just went down to *ZERO*

****

~ Haha! haha! haha!
~ Why are you laughing?
~ Look at you, Yesterday you didn't
wanted to face me because you were
so proud of your appearance. Why?
Just because you had her? Now the
same girl dumped you calling ugly
and you're like standing in front
of me for like 2 hours, lol that's
funny haha!
~ Still standing (Speechless)!

# A conversation between me and my reflection in mirror.

You talk about humans killing
humans?
That's a pity small topic, because;

Humanity killed
Equality killed
Education killed
Environment killed
Eco system killed
Respect killed
Love killed
Trust killed
Faith killed
And
World kill...(on the verge)
I'm afraid if it turns
"World killed"

# Karma!

You know what I love the most about
this word,
It doesn't check anyone's CAST,
STATUS, RELIGION, POWER, POSITION,
GENDER, RACE and NATIONALITY.
It works for all class of people.
KARMA, totally Impartial and Non-
discriminative word.

****

# My 2am thoughts..

Nights are as usual, silence is as
usual, everything is as usual.
Then what is that unusual which is
haunting me?????? Unusual of this
haunted night is that I miss her
and can't talk to her, I wish to
see her smile but can't make A
video call , today's unusuality is
I don't get that loving Good night
texts from her when I sleep,
unusual is that I wake up at odd
timings with her thoughts only,
unusually my hearts cries for love
and miss her warm embrace,

unusually there's fully silence inside me and I'm searching noise outside, unusually I sleep back again with her pictures in my lifeless hands. Oh God I hate this Unusuality, why can't things get usual, why can't I call her waking up at odd timings? Why are my hands shivering while touching her face in her portraits?. Why can't things get usual so that I don't need to search noise in this silence. Why can't things just be as usual as it used to be.

Oh God, I just hate this "Unusuality!"
Somewhere between you and me, we lost us.

# I'm a total mess up

My hearts doesn't co-ordinate my actions, my actions don't co-ordinate my eyes, my eyes don't co-ordinate my dreams, my dreams don't co-ordinate my work, my work doesn't co-ordinate my actions, and the cycle continues.

I'm a total mess up.

He was obsessed with extra time work in office, Returning back home, her one smile was enough to heal his obsession. Yes, Mother's love is always so precious.

# Amrita Kour

Amrita kour daughter of Mr. Narender pal singh and Rajvinder kaur was born in Delhi and brought up in Rourkela, Odisha. She is 23 years old and currently running a small business of clothing and a part time tutor. Apart from her business and studies she work as a content writer for different firms. She is very passionate and her passion makes her to caliber and strives to make her parents proud. Writing is her deep heart feeling and passion as well as a source of happiness from last one year. She loves to realte her writing with the experience of life and reality. She is also co-author of many Anthologies ( Miracles from heaven, Blissful reminiscing soul, kissa-e-zindagi, etc....) . Let's hope for positive and encouraging response and love for her writings from your side.

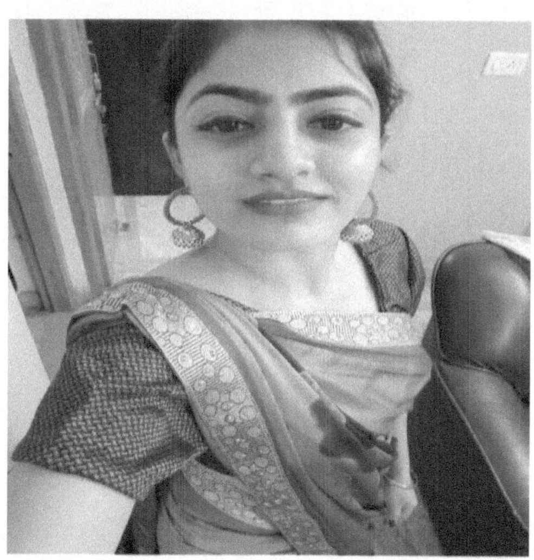

# "Proud to be a girl"

Yes, I am a girl and

I am proud to be a girl.

I am a girl and I am independent.

I am a girl and I can take
responsibility of my family.

I am a girl and I go out and handle
all my works by own.

I am a girl and I am capable of
running my own business.

I am a girl and I take all
responsibility if my parents.

I am a girl and I have my own
source of earnings.

I am a girl and yes I am very
successful in my life.

Yes, I am a Girl and I am proud to
be a Girl.

My parents are proud of me.

# "Love"

Love is beautiful feeling.

The first person who gave me unconditional love is My Mother and the second person is My Father. They both are mine whole world. I just can't imagine my life without my parents. I also have a elder sister she just a second mother to me in my life and a small brother like a child and also my crime partner. This much of love was unconditional and this makes my life beautiful. But this world has used this beautiful word love as a cheater just because of some time pass relationship. If you really wanna know what is love just go and spent time with your family and you will get to know what the love is and what does that mean and how this love spread happiness in every situation whether it's good or worst, doesn't matter. But you will always find your parents with you and they will be with you till the last breathe. Love you mom and dad.

# Independence

I am a girl and I have all Independence in my life, but still in today's generation there are many families who don't even trust their girls. They don't allow them to go outside, they don't even allow them to study, always the family is treating the girl like a burden , always a girl has been taught how to sit, how to stand whom to talk and whom not to talk . Girls shouldn't go there, she can't stay outside for late night, she has to come home before 6pm, she has learned to wake up early, and she must learn all the household works. Why the family doesn't teach their son that what is manner how sit, how to walk, and how to talk with girl, how to respect a girl. They must be taught this. If all these things got learnt by a boy than no rapes, no harassment case will be file... Girls can move out freely, girls can hangout with their friends, girls can move out for movies ... Girls can go out for job ... Girls will be safe. But this all we think and rest all only watch out the scenes happening , no one will come forward to hello out but everyone is ready to give the suggestion , no one will make this taught successful but everyone is ready to pin out.

I must just if I could get a chance than I must be there for every girl... I must teach lesson to every boy, I must hang to the death all the rapist... Every girl must get all the right which boys are getting.

# Depth of soul

"Soul" when one soul gives birth to another soul and that soul will be very lucky if it gives birth to a baby girl child. And when a mother gives a birth to a new life, that mother also get a new life because that labor pain is unbearable , its like the mother have came back from the heavens of God. But after looking to the child she gave birth all the pain which she has beared that all get wipe out of the mind and never get reminds of it, because the child gift is very precious in the life of a women . Its just priceless to see her child after 9 months . A mother love is priceless because she loves her child without seeing the child , without knowing the child color. The day she got to know that she will become a mom one day from that moment she gives unconditional love to the child and bear all the discomfort and pain for her child. Because a mother can do anything for her children happiness. We girls are very luck that we have got such a beautiful power that we can give birth to a soul and that soul will be our child. Most precious gift she gets if she birth to a baby girl. Its just said to be a precious gift of Laxmi goddess. That parents feels so lucky to have their first baby as a baby girls in the form of their love. They take cares of that baby like a princess ... Gives all the happiness and makes always smile to her ... But its very difficult face of life when you have fix a marriage of your daughter . It feels like some one has taken a part of your soul from you. Its very hard to send your daughter to the house of in laws. Because no can take of her like princess like you did from the birth to the marriage . And that daughter also have questions in the mind that why a girl has to leave there parents after the marriage , why she can't live with them after marriage. That phase of life changes everything. "Yes i am a girl, my parents are proud of me ."

www.ingramcontent.com/pod-product-compliance
Lightning Source LLC
LaVergne TN
LVHW091234180726
843490LV00006B/2071